CW01083000

To Alice H.

William Heinemann Ltd
10 Upper Grosvenor Street
London W1X 9PA
LONDON MELBOURNE
AUCKLAND JOHANNESBURG
Published in Great Britain 1986
Copyright © 1986 Jenny Partridge
ISBN 0 434 95683 X
Printed in Hong Kong by
Mandarin Offset Marketing (H.K.) Ltd.

Clara Quince

JENNY PARTRIDGE

HEINEMANN : LONDON

"Mint tea, sugar, clothes pegs, indigestion powder." Clara Quince, shrew and housekeeper to Colonel Grunt, peered at the crumpled shopping list as she followed the path to Pollensnuff Stores.

To get into the shop she had to squeeze past a group of young woodlanders who were looking at a poster on the door announcing the Country Fair.

Once inside, she gave the list to Mrs
Pollensnuff and sat down on a stool.
"I see there's to be a Fair on Saturday,"
  she said.
"Yes," said Mrs Pollensnuff. "The little

ones are busy making costumes for the
fancy dress parade. I hope you will be
bringing some of your special elderflower
and gooseberry jelly again this year, Miss
Quince?"

Clara smiled as she remembered the fairs
of long ago, when she and her brothers
had played on the roundabouts and

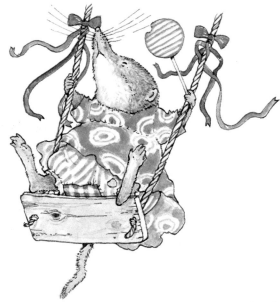

swings. She recalled how excited she had
been when she won a whole jar of
coloured lollipops, and the fun she had
secretly peeping through a gap in the
fortune-teller's tent.

"Pah, elderflower and gooseberry jam,"
she said picking up her basket. "I think I
can do better than that!" And she hurried

out of the shop leaving Mrs Pollensnuff to
puzzle out what she meant.

"You've forgotten the indigestion
powder," she called after her, but Clara
had gone.

Back at Mayfly Manor, Colonel Grunt
complained that Clara had not brought
his indigestion powder and hiccuped all
through supper. When the table had been

cleared and the plates washed and put
back on the dresser, Clara crept up to the
attic. She blew the dust and cobwebs off
the old wooden chest which stood by the
wall and looked inside.

She pulled out several lace tablecloths,
nine curtain rings and a cracked goldfish
bowl, took them downstairs to the
kitchen and talked to Tarquin about her
marvellous idea for the Fair. He was busy
toasting muffins and told her she should
get on with her jam making. But instead,
Clara fetched her sewing basket and set
to work. She was going to have fun!

Saturday was sunny and everyone in
Oakapple Wood was out enjoying the
Fair. Little mice giggled as they queued
up outside the mysterious fortune-teller's
tent, jingling their pocket money.

Grandma Snuffles joined the queue,
dragging a reluctant Mr Squint with her.
The crowd grew larger and Madam
Columbine, the Fortune Teller, looked
pleased as she awaited her first customer.

MADAM
COLUMBINE
FORTUNES
TOLD
5

QUEUE

"You must beware of a strange
three-legged creature with two heads,"
she warned Mr Squint. How amazed he

was when he stepped outside the tent and
collided with Amy and Pippin who had
just been running in the three-legged
race!

Colonel Grunt was the next customer.
Madam Columbine gazed into her
crystal ball and told him that if he looked
inside his ear trumpet all his troubles
would be over.
"Good gracious me," he said, pulling out a
packet of indigestion powder.

Grandma Snuffles sat down and peered eagerly at the fortune-teller. "What do you see in your crystal ball for me?" she asked.

"For you, I see a pot of gold," said Madam
Columbine. Grandma Snuffles was
delighted – she couldn't believe her ears.

Outside, everyone was talking about the mysterious Madam Columbine. Who could she be? Where did she come from?

At that moment the tent opened and the fortune-teller came out. There were gasps from the crowd as she took off her veil and headscarf.

"Why, it's Clara!" said Colonel Grunt.
Clara laughed so much that all her
bracelets and rings jingled.
"But where is my pot of gold?" demanded
Grandma Snuffles.

Still smiling, Clara took a small jar
from her pocket. On it was written
"Madam Columbine's Elderflower
and Gooseberry Jelly". Now everyone
laughed, even Grandma Snuffles!

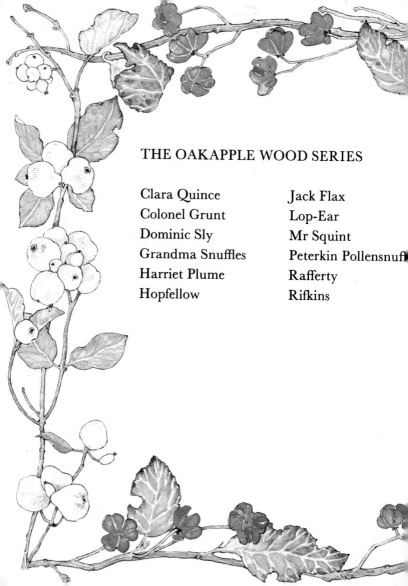

THE OAKAPPLE WOOD SERIES